RATCHET & CLANK

THE OFFICIAL GUIDE

By Josh Richardson

Based on characters created by
Insomniac Games

Scholastic Inc.

Published by Scholastic Inc., *Publishers since 1920.* SCHOLASTIC and associated logos are trademarks and/or registered trademarks of Scholastic Inc.

ISBN 978-1-338-04549-9

10 9 8 7 6 5 4 3 2 1   16 17 18 19 20

Printed in the U.S.A.   40

First printing 2016

CONTENTS

SECTION 1
INTRODUCTION

GREETINGS!

Have you ever dreamed of exploring the stars, going on crazy adventures, meeting strange new life-forms, and maybe even saving the galaxy?

Ever since they became Galactic Rangers, best buds Ratchet and Clank have been living that dream. Their journey has taken them across the galaxy—from the lava fields of Gaspar to the lush tropical islands of Pokitaru and beyond. Together, they've come up against some of the meanest bad guys in the cosmos.

The universe is a really big place full of wonders and dangers beyond your wildest imagination. This book is the definitive guide through the *Ratchet & Clank* universe, filled with insider info usually reserved for high-ranking Galactic Rangers. Learn about all the heroes and villains, check out the inner workings of Ratchet and Clank's many gadgets and weapons, and take a tour of the galaxy through the eyes of our unlikely heroes!

Are you ready to start your own intergalactic journey? Then go ahead—turn the page!

SECTION 2
MEET THE HEROES

When chasing bad guys across the universe, it's really important to have your friends there to cover your back! In this section, you'll get to know more about our two main heroes and their friends. Learn more about where Ratchet and Clank came from and how they became inseparable. Meet the Galactic Rangers, and check out some of the friends Ratchet and Clank meet across the galaxy.

2

MEET THE HEROES

An expert mechanic with a kind heart and a love for adventure, Ratchet dreams of becoming a Galactic Ranger and doing big things with his life. He lives in the Kyzil Plateau region of the planet Veldin with his friend Grim, who raised Ratchet since he was a baby. Ratchet likes Grim and his job at Grim's garage, but he can't help feeling drawn to the stars.

When the Galactic Rangers announced they were holding tryouts to find a new member for their team, Ratchet leapt at the opportunity. Thanks to his natural acrobatic abilities and fantastic skill with gadgets and weapons, he aced the test. However, Captain Qwark and the other Rangers were not impressed. They rejected Ratchet's application because of some careless mistakes he'd made in the past, including "possession of an illegal gravity repulsor" and "willful disruption of the space-time continuum."

Even though he didn't join the Rangers, Ratchet's life changed forever that same night. He spotted a spaceship crash near his home, and he used his swingshot to reach the crash site, where he pulled a tiny robot from the wreckage. Although he didn't know it at the time, that robot would soon become his best friend and companion on an adventure that would span the galaxy and make Ratchet's biggest dreams come true...

THE HERO

Small in size but big on brainpower and heart, Clank is nothing like the mindless machine of mayhem he was meant to be.

Clank was created in Chairman Drek's warbot factory on the planet Quartu when a bolt of lightning caused a temporary glitch in the assembly line. Instead of creating a hulking warbot intent on killing the Galactic Rangers, the glitch made a tiny robot who wanted to save the Rangers!

Chairman Drek ordered his robotic bodyguard, Victor, to chase down and destroy this "defective" warbot. Clank used his small size and super smarts to outwit Victor and escape in a Blarg scout ship. But Victor managed to damage the ship with a rocket blast at the last second, sending Clank on a crash course to the planet Veldin.

After Ratchet rescued him, Clank happily teamed up with his newfound friend on a mission to save the galaxy.

CLANK'S WARBOT NAME IS B5429A.

FAST FRIENDS

Investigating a mysterious spaceship crash near his home, Ratchet saved a tiny robot from the wreckage seconds before the spaceship's engines exploded. When Ratchet tried examining the robot for signs of damage, it sprang back to life and tried to hobble away...only to fall flat on its face.

"An army is coming, and I must warn them!" the tiny warbot cried.

Ratchet knelt down to help. "Hang on, slow down, you've been in a crash! What do you say we get you back to my garage. I'll run a diagnostic and have you fixed up in no time."

The tiny robot took a moment to ponder his situation. "Thank you, I appreciate the assistance."

"It's no problem," Ratchet said. "So, what do I call you?"

The tiny robot tried to take a few steps on his damaged leg. "I suppose...*CLANK*...my official...*CLANK*...warbot designation is..." Then he fell flat on his face again.

Ratchet laughed and helped his new pal up again. "Maybe I'll just call you Clank. My name's Ratchet."

"Pleased to meet you," Clank said. The two soon-to-be heroes shook hands, beginning a friendship that would change the galaxy.

SAVING THE GALACTIC RANGERS

Ratchet and Clank raced to Aleero City to warn the Galactic Rangers of Chairman Drek's evil plans, only to find the Galactic Rangers Headquarters had been overrun with Blarg and warbots!

Clank used the Magnebooster on their ship to pick up swarms of warbots while Ratchet steered them toward the Blarg warship. Clank turned off the Magnebooster at just the right moment, using the warbots as makeshift missiles to destroy the warship and save the Rangers.

BREAKING INTO DREK INDUSTRIES

After starting their assault on Drek Industries, the Galactic Rangers found the front door locked. Luckily, there was a nearby air vent just big enough for Clank to fit through.

Clank used his smarts to reprogram Gadgebots, transforming them into springs, power supplies, and bridges that helped him reach the door controls and let the Rangers inside to continue their mission.

STOPPING DR. NEFARIOUS

Ratchet and Clank put all of their skills to the test during their final battle with Dr. Nefarious and his gigantic Gadgetron Instamech.

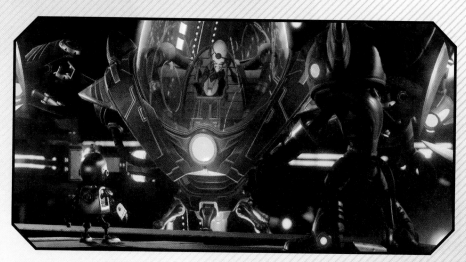

Clank transformed into the Jetpack, allowing Ratchet to stay airborne when Dr. Nefarious smashed the platforms they were standing on.

Meanwhile, Ratchet used all of the weapons at his disposal to bring down Dr. Nefarious for good!

GALACTIC RANGERS

Champions of justice, the Galactic Rangers represent the best of the best of the best in the entire universe. Led by the charismatic Captain Qwark and equipped with the latest in high-tech weaponry, the Rangers are never afraid to tackle threats to galactic peace. Ratchet looks up to the Galactic Rangers and dreams of joining them on their adventures.

CAPTAIN QWARK

Captain Qwark is the leader of the Galactic Rangers and public face of the team. The only thing bigger than his bulging muscles is his massive ego. He adores bragging about his heroics on galactic social media. He pretends to be brave and strong in front of the camera, but in reality, Captain Qwark is a scaredy-cat who would do anything for fame or money.

CORA VERALUX

Cora Veralux is the youngest Galactic Ranger, specializing in finding trouble and then kicking it in the rear. She's definitely a "shoot first, ask questions later" kind of gal, preferring to enter a fight with guns blazing instead of listening to Elaris's detailed strategies.

CORA UP6 BORN ON
THE PLANET KOVPLE6.

BRAX LECTRUS

Brax "The Brute" Lectrus started his career as a professional wrestler, quickly gaining fame after his performance at Grapplemania. Now a Galactic Ranger, Brax loves to jump into the heat of battle and get hands-on with his enemies.

ELARIS

Elaris is the Galactic Rangers' science officer, in charge of developing new gear and providing technical support on their missions. She's one of the smartest people in the galaxy. Elaris and Clank enjoy working together to find solutions to challenges the Rangers face.

GRIMROTH RAZZ

Grim is the owner of the spaceship repair business where Ratchet works as a mechanic. Many years ago, he found a baby Lombax left at the front door of his garage. Grim took in the baby and raised him, naming him "Ratchet" after his gift for fixing machines.

Grim might seem like the grumpy type at first glance, but he's really a kindhearted and hardworking soul who always has Ratchet's best interests at heart. He always knows the right thing to say to inspire Ratchet to reach his potential—like, "To be a hero, you don't have to do big things, just the right ones."

FELTON RAZZ

Although the resemblance is uncanny, Felton Razz is nothing like his brother Grim. A "professional chillaxer," Felton avoids hard work and loves to relax and fish at his home on the planet Pokitaru.

Ratchet and Clank meet Felton when their fight against Chairman Drek and his Blargian forces reaches Pokitaru. Felton helps the duo navigate the planet and stop the Blarg from stealing all of Pokitaru's water.

BIG AL

In addition to being the galaxy's greatest electronics expert, Big Al is an all-around super nerd. He owns a store called Roboshack in Aleero City, is a fan of comic books, and likes to attend comic conventions in his spare time. Big Al is always happy to help the Galactic Rangers in a time of need.

Ratchet and Clank first meet Big Al in Aleero City when Drek's warbots assault the Galactic Ranger HQ. He installs a Helipack upgrade for Clank to increase the duo's aerial mobility. Their next meeting is on Pokitaru, where Big Al upgrades Clank with a Thrusterpack and equips the team's ship with powerful Tesla Blast Rockets.

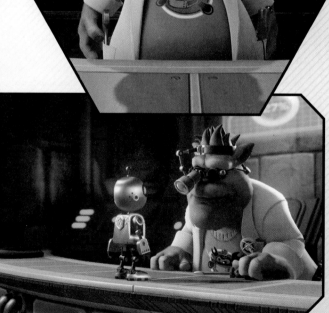

THE PLUMBER

The Plumber is in charge of maintaining the Waterworks in Novalis Valley. He's pretty great at fixing things that are broken, and it's rumored that he can see into the future as well.

Ratchet and Clank first encountered The Plumber on Novalis, where their spaceship had crashed after being shot down by Blargian warships. The two heroes rescued the mayor of Novalis Valley, and to thank them, The Plumber happily fixed their craft.

SKIDD McMARX

Skidd McMarx is the nephew of the mayor of Novalis Valley and the most famous professional hoverboard racer in the galaxy. Ratchet is a big fan of Skidd McMarx and is eager to help his idol when he learns Skidd had run into some trouble on the planet Aridia.

Although Skidd is a hoverboard champion, he's not the brightest when it comes to business. His dishonest manager often takes advantage of Skidd, using the professional hoverboarder's fame to grow his own fortunes.

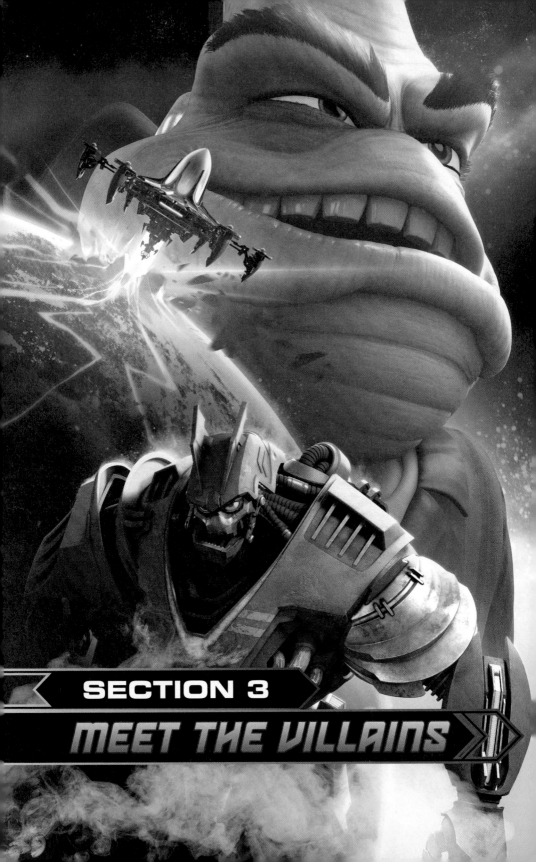

SECTION 3
MEET THE VILLAINS

Corrupt, immoral, and just all-around evil, these dastardly villains are some of the worst the galaxy has to offer. These guys will stop at nothing to achieve their selfish plans, no matter who might get hurt along the way.

Take a good look through this rogues' gallery and know thy enemy—it might just save your bacon one day!

CHAIRMAN DREK ≫

Chairman Alonzo Drek is the head honcho at Drek Industries, an evil corporation headquartered on the Blarg home world, Quartu. Bold, brash, and evil to the bone, Chairman Drek believes the universe is his for the taking and that no one can stop his maniacal plans. Fear keeps his employees in line, as Chairman Drek has been known to punish his workers for minor annoyances like texting during a meeting.

Chairman Drek's small size forces him to use a scooter to move from place to place. He also relies heavily on his minions to do his dirty work, including his assistant, Zed, and robotic bodyguard, Victor Von Ion. Drek is also responsible for breaking Dr. Nefarious out of prison and employing Nefarious's evil genius to make his darkest desires come true.

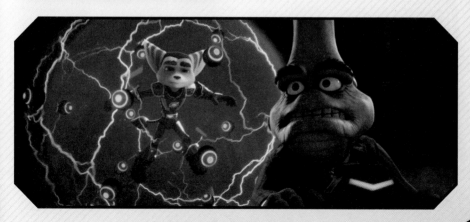

Zed is Chairman Drek's personal assistant. He handles most of the administrative tasks at Drek Industries. Never very far from Drek's side, Zed does his best to keep up with his boss's demands, no matter how crazy they may seem. He is the definition of a "yes" man (or robot, in Zed's case). After all, a happy boss is a boss who's less likely to deactivate you.

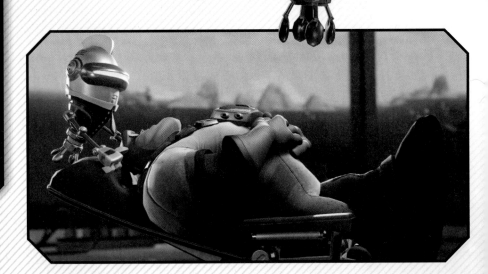

ꙅƎD ꞃꙅꞀ ꞇꙅꞃ꭯Ɓ ꞇꙅꞃ ꞓꞃꙅꝅꞏ

Zed isn't the smartest robot on the block, and he's no match for Clank's superior processing power. His loyalty to Chairman Drek isn't absolute either—after being captured by the Galactic Rangers, he quickly gives up the details of his boss's evil plans. To Zed, this job was only supposed to be temporary until he gets his singing career on track.

VICTOR VON ION

Underneath Victor Von Ion's cold metal exterior is the motherboard of a savage warrior. Unlike the mass-produced warbots from Drek's factory, Victor is a self-aware being with his own thoughts and desires. As Chairman Drek's personal bodyguard, Victor is often sent on missions to deal with problems that require his special brand of brutality.

Victor is equipped with a high-powered laser that can cut through the toughest materials and an arm-mounted energy blade used for close combat situations. He also carries a rocket launcher as his personal sidearm. Despite his impressive arsenal and combat skills, Victor has one major design flaw: He isn't waterproof. Any exposure to water will rust his frame, causing him to short circuit and fall over.

None of Chairman Drek's plans could be realized without Dr. Nefarious, who is the very definition of an evil genius. He is responsible for designing and creating the warbots, the Deplanetizer, and all the weapons used by those in Drek's employ. Chairman Drek believes he controls Dr. Nefarious, but in reality it's the other way around! Nefarious is only using Drek and his vast resources to achieve his own goals: the destruction of the Galactic Rangers and control over the universe.

What few people know is Dr. Nefarious was once a member of the Galactic Rangers, and he created most of the weapons and gadgets they use today. The Rangers drove Dr. Nefarious to madness—they forced him to work without a proper laboratory, and he was relentlessly teased by Captain Qwark. Now his hunger for revenge threatens to tear the galaxy apart.

MANY USED TO CALL DR. NEFARIOUS THE
"KING OF THE KERS MERS."

MEET THE VILLAINS

3

The Blarg come from the planet Quartu, and nearly all of them work for Chairman Drek at Drek Industries. As a group, the Blarg are very weak willed and easily manipulated by fear of getting on Chairman Drek's bad side. During their adventures, Ratchet and Clank encounter a variety of Blarg soldiers.

BLARG SCOUT TROOPERS

Blarg scout troopers are the majority of Drek's forces. Ratchet can easily take these guys down with just his OmniWrench.

BLARG SNIPERS

Blarg snipers are equipped with aim-assist helmets that help them land long-range shots.

BLARG HEAVY TROOPERS

Blarg heavy troopers are equipped with some serious firepower. Luckily, Ratchet and Clank have an impressive arsenal of their own to take these guys down.

Built from the finest Raritanium in the galaxy and programmed with every offensive tactic in the Galactic Rangers handbook, warbots are the latest addition to Chairman Drek's army. They are assembled in a massive factory designed by Dr. Nefarious, and their only objective is to destroy.

3

MEET THE VILLAINS

The warbots come equipped with heavy armor and powerful weapons. Some warbots also tote packs that give them limited flight abilities.

Ratchet and Clank must carefully dodge their shots before counterattacking.

Thankfully, warbots are not very smart, making it easy to fool them with gadgets like the Hologuise.

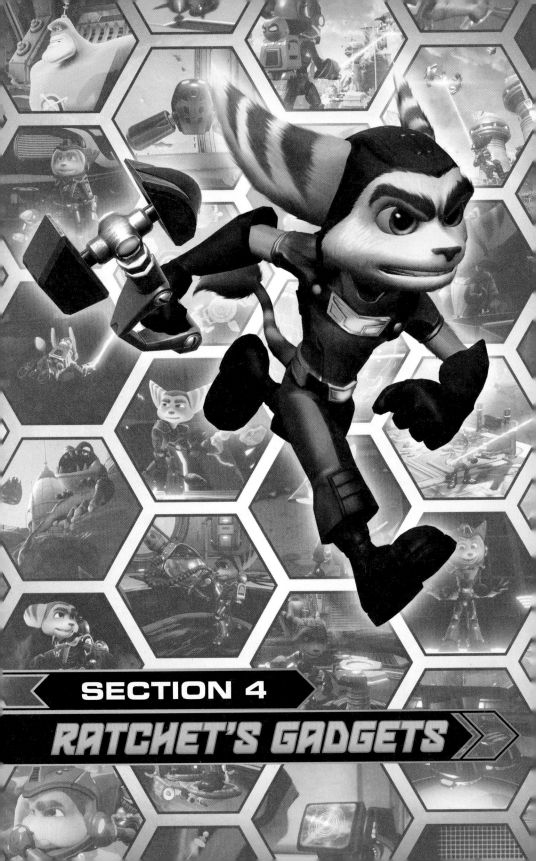

SECTION 4
RATCHET'S GADGETS

Ratchet knows a mechanic isn't much use to anyone without the right set of tools. Thankfully, this Lomba is always equipped with the proper gadget for whatever might come his way.

From the ever-reliable OmniWrench 8000 to the top-of-the-line Galactic Ranger protosuit, this section gives a good look at each of Ratchet's gadgets and how he uses them in the field.

⬡ OMNIWRENCH 8000 ≫

Ratchet would never be caught without his handy and reliable OmniWrench 8000, which he's used since he was a child. Ratchet's so skilled at using this tool, he can throw it like a boomerang! Aside from fixing up spaceships, this trusty OmniWrench can be used in a number of different ways:

Bashing open crates to collect all those shiny bolts hidden inside!

Turning those bolt switches and opening up new areas!

Smacking nasty aliens in the head and sending them home crying!

THE OMNIWRENCH 8000 IS ALSO GREAT FOR TAKING SHORTCUTS OUT OF THE OVEN.

SWINGSHOT

The swingshot is an energy-based grappling hook Ratchet uses to cross large gaps. Ratchet fires a small claw device that's stored in his glove, and an energy rope shoots out and attaches to compatible versa-targets.

HOVERBOARD

Given to Ratchet by the legendary Skidd McMarx, this hoverboard allows Ratchet to compete in races on the planets Rilgar and Kalebo III.

Ratchet's natural agility helps him pull off wicked stunts on the Rilgar hoverboard track.

HYDRODISPLACER

Fish can breathe underwater, but a Lombax doesn't have the luxury of gills to help him travel through flooded passageways. Thankfully, the Hydrodisplacer can help clear a path. Take a look at this excerpt from the Hydrodisplacer user's manual to learn how it works:

> *This device, when hooked up to a receptacle, grabs and removes all the excess space in between atoms to compress nearly any size body of liquid into the device to be transported to any location and released into another receptacle.*

Basically, this is just a fancy way of saying the Hydrodisplacer can move large amounts of water. A very useful tool for navigating the sewers of Rilgar!

⚙ TRESPASSER ≫

Ratchet uses the Trespasser whenever he needs to break into an electronic door lock or hack into computer systems. The Trespasser uses advanced poly-laser technology to hack internal photon receptors and bypass these security locks.

This is accomplished by rotating circular dials to align the poly-lasers with all the red photon receptors, but be careful not to block any of the beams! Some computer systems are harder to crack than others, but luckily Elaris can upgrade the Trespasser with an auto-hack upgrade Ratchet can use if he gets stumped.

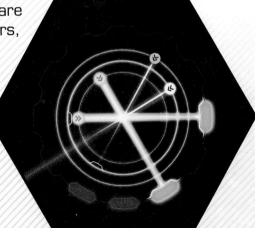

BOX BREAKER

The Box Breaker is an upgrade to the OmniWrench 8000 that allows Ratchet to collect bolts more efficiently. After performing a jumping slam attack with the OmniWrench 8000, the Box Breaker emits a wide-radius shockwave of compressed air, which sucks in bolts from far away at high speed.

Ratchet gets this upgrade on the planet Gaspar after helping a friendly Blarg scientist complete his collection of Telepathopus brains.

MAP-O-MATIC

Hidden away at the end of a secret grind rail path at the Gadgetron Headquarters on Kelebo III, the Map-O-Matic upgrades the map display in Ratchet's suit. By tuning into a specific frequency of atomic excitement, the Map-O-Matic automatically marks the locations of hidden raritanium, Golden Bolts, and Holocard packs.

The Galactic Rangers are equipped with the best gear in the universe, and it all starts with the protosuit. As the most advanced combat armor on the market, the protosuit is built for protecting the Rangers in all sorts of dangerous situations.

The protosuit helmet contains a neural sensor that reads the user's thoughts, then instantly teleports the desired weapon into his or her hands. It also contains a heads-up display that is used to convey mission info and track enemy movement. Plus, it lets the Rangers breathe in outer space.

Galactic Ranger protosuits also come standard with propulsion jets, but these have been removed on Ratchet's protosuit to make room for Clank. Thankfully, with some help from Big Al, Clank can use his versa-motors to compensate for the loss in mobility.

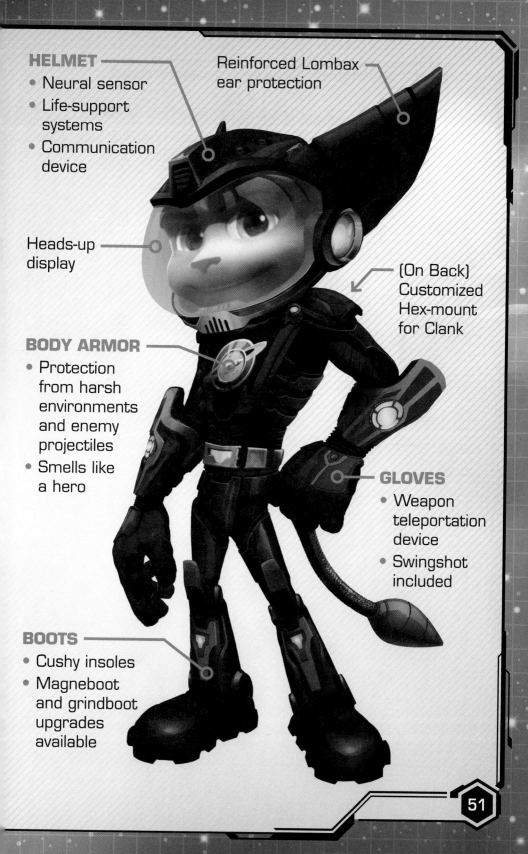

HELMET
- Neural sensor
- Life-support systems
- Communication device

Reinforced Lombax ear protection

Heads-up display

(On Back) Customized Hex-mount for Clank

BODY ARMOR
- Protection from harsh environments and enemy projectiles
- Smells like a hero

GLOVES
- Weapon teleportation device
- Swingshot included

BOOTS
- Cushy insoles
- Magneboot and grindboot upgrades available

GRINDBOOTS

ound deep in the heart of a Blarg research station on Gaspar, Grindboots allow Ratchet to skate effortlessly along grind rails throughout the galaxy.

Ratchet can jump and attack while using the Grindboots. He can also hit switches along his path or leap to another nearby grind rail to dodge dangers.

MAGNEBOOTS

Upgrading the protosuit with Magneboots allows Ratchet to walk up walls and along ceilings that are covered by special "magnesurfaces."

These gravity-defying surfaces can be spotted by their distinct hexagon grid pattern. These paths usually lead to hidden goodies!

The standard Galactic Ranger helmet may keep a Ranger breathing in the depths of space, but its life-support systems don't apply underwater. Without the O_2 Mask, Ratchet can only stay underwater for a short amount of time before he has to come back up for air.

Once Ratchet finds this upgrade hidden away on the resort planet Pokitaru, he can stay underwater for as long as he pleases!

HOLOGUISE

When the need arises to appear like someone else, look no further than the Gadgetron Hologuise! Ratchet used this gadget to disguise himself as Captain Qwark in order to fool Drek's warbots and sneak into the core of the Deplanetizer.

Warbots are as dumb as they are dangerous, so they simply let Ratchet pass by without raising any alarms.

SECTION 5
CLANK'S UPGRADES

Clank is more than just a collection of processors and servomotors. With the help of a few upgrades, Clank can reconfigure his body to help his partner swim faster, jump higher, and even take flight!

Read on to discover the various upgrades Clank acquires during his journey. You'll become a robot expert in no time!

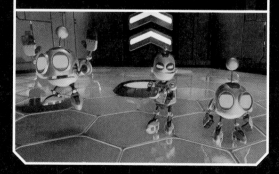

HYDROPACK

n his Hydropack configuration, Clank's arms transform into powerful turbines. The blades of the turbines work like a boat's propellers, enabling him and Ratchet to glide effortlessly through water. Clank has this ability at the start of his adventures with Ratchet.

HELIPACK

The Helipack is the first upgrade Clank receives from Big Al. With it, Clank produces powerful propellers from his hands and the top of his head so he and Ratchet can jump higher and glide safely across large distances.

THRUSTERPACK

The second upgrade Clank gets from Big Al is the Thrusterpack. It improves on the Helipack in nearly every way, replacing the three propellers of the Helipack with wings and jet thrusters! This allows Ratchet and Clank to make higher jumps and leap forward at extreme speed.

When used with the OmniWrench 8000, the Thrusterpack is powerful enough to crank up Clank's thruster turbines, opening up new areas for the duo to explore.

JET PACK

After helping a friendly Blarg scientist, Clank receives the ultimate upgrade for his versa-motors, allowing them to transform into a fully functional jet pack! With the jet pack, Ratchet and Clank can take to the skies to reach the highest of places or fight foes in the air.

Clank can't fly forever. The jet pack has limited fuel, so Ratchet needs to stand on a fueling station to refill Clank's energy reserves when they're low.

CLANK'S UPGRADES

The Gadgebots are neat little robots that can be programmed to take one of three different forms—Springbot, Powerbot, and Bridgebot. Each one is designed to perform a single specific task. Clank encounters Gadgebots frequently when adventuring on his own. He uses their unique characteristics to solve any puzzle blocking his path.

SPRINGBOT

The bouncy Springbot is ready to help Clank jump up onto high platforms. Simply leap onto his built-in platform and watch this Gadgebot spring into action!

 ## POWERBOT

The Powerbot is full of energy and ready to power up inactive doors and switches. Toss the little guy near a power converter, and his shocking personality should have Clank moving along in no time.

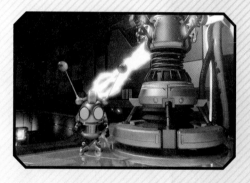

BRIDGEBOT

Crossing large gaps is no long stretch for Clank when there's a Bridgebot nearby. When deployed across a gap, the Bridgebot automatically extends and unfolds its body to create a stable bridge, letting Clank reach the other side with ease.

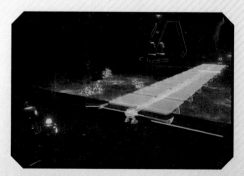

SECTION 6

THE ARMORY

Galactic Rangers explore the galaxy and defend the weak on a regular basis, but the best part of the job is all the fun weapons they get to use in action!

Ratchet earns experience with each weapon, gaining levels as he becomes increasingly familiar with how to use them. When Ratchet reaches level five with a specific weapon, it morphs into a new and more destructive version.

New weapons are purchased from Gadgetron vendors using the many bolts  Ratchet and Clank pick up during their adventures. Gadgetron vendors can also upgrade any weapon using raritanium , thus increasing the weapon's combat potential.

6

Although it may look tempting, don't practice juggling with Fusion Grenades! These little spheres of destruction explode on contact when thrown at enemies or objects, releasing a cluster of Pyrocidic Nitroballs that burn right through enemy armor.

MAX LEVEL: FUSION BOMB

Functionally, the Fusion Bomb works exactly like the Fusion Grenade, but this puppy packs more Pyrocidic Nitroballs into the same package. That means bigger explosions and greater damage!

RARITANIUM UPGRADES

Frictionless Hopper: Increases rate of fire

Telehopper: Increases rate of fire

Servo-Assisted Pitch: Increases throwing range

COMBUSTER

The "backbone of the Galactic Ranger arsenal," according to Captain Qwark, the Combuster is a reliable weapon in most combat situations. It fires burning balls of plasma that deal a light amount of damage, but its impressive ammo storage means it can fire many times before running dry.

MAX LEVEL: MAGMABUSTER

The Magmabuster fires three projectiles at once in a spread pattern. A thermal prism installed in the plasma injector superheats the shots and creates the extra projectiles.

RARITANIUM UPGRADES

BOGO Plasma: Doubles ammo capacity

Heavy Plasma: Shots can stun enemies

Stable Plasma: Shots travel farther

PYROCITOR >>

Commonly known as a flamethrower, the Pyrocitor fires a steady stream of burning Pyrocidic fluid. It's a smart choice for keeping enemies from invading Ratchet's personal space—and it's great for barbecuing hot dogs, too!

MAX LEVEL: LAVACITOR

The Lavacitor injects Lavamorph particles into the stream of Pyrocific fluid, which causes enemies to explode when hit. Get ready to deep-fry some Blarg!

💎 RARITANIUM UPGRADES

Extradimensional Tank: Increases ammo storage capacity

Pressurized Canisters: Ammo pickups give more fuel

Lavamorph Isotopes: Explosions cause more damage

PROTON DRUM

The Proton Drum deploys a sphere-shaped core that sends out pulses of damaging subatomic energy. Ratchet can fire one of these supermassive pseudo-

atoms into a group of enemies, then switch to another weapon to deal even more damage!

MAX LEVEL: PROTOCLAST

The Protoclast adds a shocking new ability to its pseudo-atom projectiles. Charged clouds of energy emitted by the projectile mix with subatomic energy, creating arcs of lightning that automatically seek out the nearest enemy.

RARITANIUM UPGRADES

Pseudo-Quantum Particles: Increases ammo capacity

Frictionless Casing: Cores travel farther when fired

Constructive Resonator: Allows two cores to be deployed at once

Subatomic Drum Polarizer: Protoclast energy arcs can hit two targets at once

MR. ZURKON

Manufactured by GrummelNet Industries, the synthenoid known as Mr. Zurkon is programmed to protect the person who deploys him on the battlefield. Mr. Zurkon takes his job very seriously and is prone to taunting both his opponents and his operator during combat.

MAX LEVEL: ZURKON JR.

Did you know there is an entire Zurkon family? Mr. Zurkon's son, Zurkon Jr., is eager to show his dad he can take down alien threats like a big boy. If you think this father and son duo is intimidating, just imagine what Mrs. Zurkon must be like!

RARITANIUM UPGRADES

Dormancy Protocol: Hold more inactive Zurkon units in reserve

Hyperbolic Optics: Increases Mr. Zurkon's attack range

GROOVITRON

Nobody can resist a dance party, and the beats that play from the Groovitron are drop-dead funky. When deployed near a group of enemies, the Groovitron creates a disco inferno that forces any enemies within its range to dance uncontrollably.

MAX LEVEL: GROOVIBOMB

The Groovibomb turns any battlefield into a dance floor—and the Nitrofetti packed into its core makes for an explosive finale! Decorative yet devastating, these Nitrofetti particles explode once the Groovibomb hits the ground.

RARITANIUM UPGRADES

Double Disco: Two Groovitrons can be deployed at the same time

Nesting Balls: Increases ammo capacity

Nitrofetti Amplifier: Increases Groovibomb explosion radius

PIXELIZER

The Pixelizer is a close-range weapon that fires a wide blast of low-resolution energy, transforming enemies into something from an old video game! A second shot from the Pixelizer will break down enemies into tiny pixel blocks, complete with retro sound effects.

MAX LEVEL: PIXELIZER HD

The Pixelizer HD adds an expansion pack to the base weapon, allowing it to be charged until it releases the dreaded "Megablast 64" that turns practically any enemy into pixel-dust. Any additional questions about pixel-based weapons should be directed to an adult; they remember what games were like way back when.

RARITANIUM UPGRADES

Health Genie: Enemies can drop health pickups when defeated

Ammo Shark: Enemies can drop ammo pickups when defeated

Double Buffer: Increases rate of fire

PLASMA STRIKER

The Plasma Striker is a long-range sniper rifle equipped with a special bioscope that highlights enemy weak points in red. Ratchet can use the bioscope's three zoom levels to strike enemies that are too far away for other weapons to hit.

MAX LEVEL: PLASMA SLAYER

The Plasma Slayer's bioscope temporarily increases the shooter's metabolism, activating a slow-motion effect. This miracle of science gives Ratchet time to line up his shots and deal extra damage to enemy weak points.

RARITANIUM UPGRADES

Hollow Points: Increases size of enemy weak points, and shots explode on impact

Raritanium Coating: Shots pierce through enemies

Adrenal Scope: Increases slow-motion effect while aiming

W hen a Lombax just needs to blow something up right away, bring out the Warmonger. This mighty rocket launcher holds its warheads in a barrel configuration, enabling it to deliver several planet-shaking explosions in rapid succession.

MAX LEVEL: PEACEMAKER

The sales pitch for the Peacemaker can be summed up as follows: "We heard you like rockets, so we put some rockets in your rockets." Each warhead fires a flurry of Thermal Microrockets upon detonation, ensuring any enemy trying to make war won't be around to disturb the peace for very long.

RARITANIUM UPGRADES

Heavy Bearings: Increases ammo capacity

Thermal Targeting: Rockets home in on enemies

Microrocket Expansion: Fires an extra Microrocket with each Peacemaker shot

6

THE ARMORY

BUZZ BLADES

Buzz Blades are sharp, spinning discs that bounce off any surface they hit, including walls, ceilings, and enemy faces. This weapon is best used in tight spaces, where its ricochet ability can cause the most havoc.

MAX LEVEL: DOOM BLADES

Doom Blades replace the traditional projectile with lightweight blades that fly farther and hit harder. Hope the Blarg like a close shave!

RARITANIUM UPGRADES

Reinforced Blades: Blades gain an additional bounce

Blade Splitter: Blades split into two smaller blades on impact

GLOVE OF DOOM

The Glove of Doom allows Ratchet to toss out a gang of angry robotic minions. These "Agents of Doom," as they are lovingly called, seek out enemies and detonate on contact. Isn't that just the cutest?

MAX LEVEL: APOCALYPSE GLOVE

The Apocalypse Glove upgrades the Agents of Doom with rocket thrusters so they can leap at their targets. The only thing worse than a cute little explosive robot is a cute little explosive robot that can jump in your face—apocalypse POW!

RARITANIUM UPGRADES

Packing Matrix: Each grenade contains an additional Agent of Doom

Compact Casing: Adds yet another Agent of Doom to a single grenade

Multistage Rockets: Increases Agent of Doom leap distance

THE ARMORY

6

"Make wool, not war" is the motto of this weapon. Like the name implies, the Sheepinator's beam transmogrifies enemies into harmless sheep. These fuzzy friends have no interest in fighting and are content to graze on any nearby grass.

MAX LEVEL: GOATINATOR

Instead of docile sheep, the Goatinator turns enemies into a primal breed of goat. These herbivores have a bone to pick with anything not made of wool and will aggressively attack nearby enemies.

RARITANIUM UPGRADES

Fleece Capacitor: Each transmogrification sends out a shockwave that can transform other enemies

Golden Fleece: Transmogrified enemies drop more bolts when defeated

Polymorph Attack: Goat attacks can transmogrify other enemies

77

PREDATOR LAUNCHER

The Predator Launcher can fire up to four guided warheads at once. Though not as powerful per shot as the Warmonger, the multi-lock sensor array built into the Predator Launcher ensures each of its homing missiles lands right on target.

MAX LEVEL: RAPTOR LAUNCHER

Borrowing the missiles-in-missiles theme from the Peacemaker, the Raptor Launcher fires several sub-missiles from each main warhead. One can never have too many missiles when battling an army of warbots.

RARITANIUM UPGRADES

Overclocked Sensors: Fires an extra missile

Ammo Loyalty Card: Ammo crates give more ammo

Recursion Depth: Each Raptor Launcher warhead fires an extra missile

Critical Cores: Increases the size of missile explosions

RYNO

Rumor on the galactic Internet is Gadgetron created plans for a weapon so overpowered, if it were ever built, its dense hail of bullets and volleys of rockets could bring an end

to civilization. So they split up the plans and hid the pieces on nine rare Holocards spread throughout the galaxy. Not exactly the smartest plan.

MAX LEVEL: RYNO XTREME!

The RYNO Xtreme! fires slugs made of fluginium, a material known to occasionally create gigantic explosions. It also fires two rockets at once, forming the icing on this delicious cake of destruction.

RARITANIUM UPGRADES

Missile Nanocasing: Increases the size of missile explosions

Refined Fluginium: Makes massive fluginium explosions even more massive

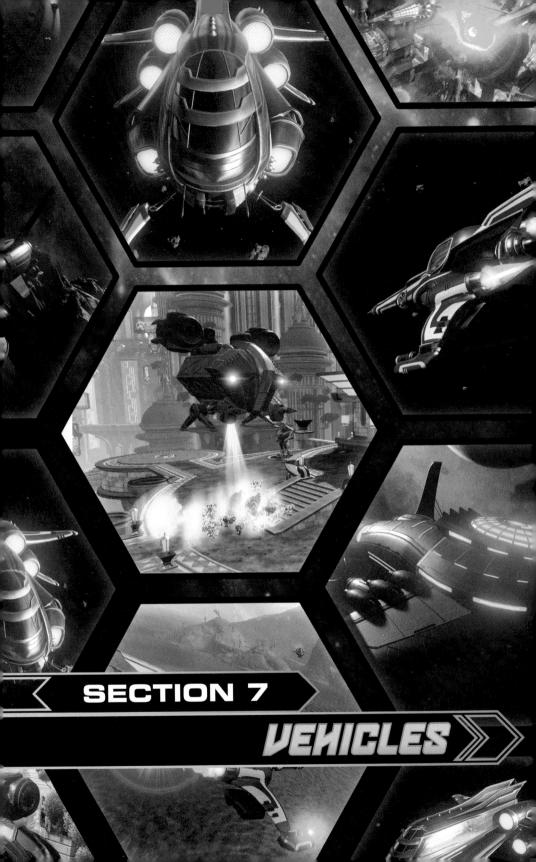

SECTION 7
VEHICLES

Going on an epic space adventure would be really tough if you didn't have a way to travel between planets, wouldn't it? Thankfully, some time ago, the aliens of the Ratchet & Clank universe figured out how to build hyperdrive engines that enable faster-than-light travel.

Turn the page and take a closer look at a few of the vehicles our heroes, and villains, use to travel the cosmos!

GALACTIC RANGERS

Our heroes can set a course and travel light-years across the galaxy at a moment's notice. And with how cool the Galactic Ranger ships look, our heroes get to travel in style, too.

STARSHIP PHOENIX

The Starship *Phoenix* serves as the Galactic Ranger's home base while out on assignment. It can reach any planet in the galaxy in record time, thanks to its ultra-powerful hyperdrive engine, and it has enough firepower to take on an entire fleet of Blarg ships.

CLASS-G STAR JUMPER

The nimble Class-G Star Jumper is the signature fighter craft of the Galactic Rangers. It's equipped with its own hyperdrive unit for interstellar travel and powerful thrusters for ship-on-ship combat. In battle, Star Jumper pilots can utilize its laser cannons against lightly armored foes or fire devastating homing rockets in situations that call for a bit more firepower.

THE BLARG

The Blarg may not be the smartest species in the galaxy, but they definitely have the capability to move large numbers of troops across the universe and deliver as much destruction as possible.

BLARG WARSHIP

The pride of the Blargian fleet, the Blarg Warship is a heavily armored space vessel capable of massive destruction. What few know is that this Warship was also built to convert into a luxury hotel in times of peace. However, the Blarg are always in a state of war, so the caches of exfoliating soaps and lavender shampoos sit unused in its cargo holds.

X6Z DROPSHIP

Also known as "The Dropship of Death," the X6Z Dropship is the workhorse of the Blargian fleet. It is used to shuttle Blarg troopers, warbots, and equipment down to a planet's surface. Troops are deployed via special teleporters mounted on the bottom of the ship's hull.

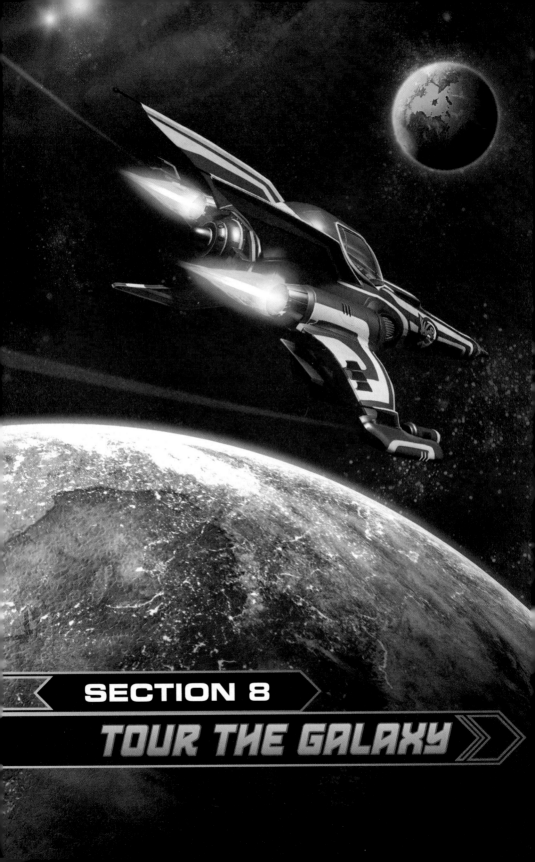

SECTION 8
TOUR THE GALAXY

On this tour of the galaxy, you'll meet exciting new alien species and experience wonders you've only dreamed about! Follow Ratchet and Clank's adventure across the cosmos, and explore the many wonders—and dangers—our heroes have encountered during their travels.

Please keep all hands, feet, and tentacles inside the ride at all times.

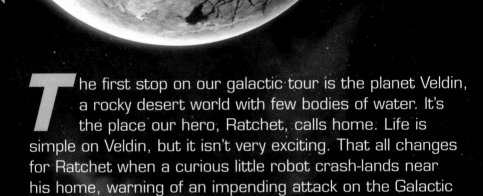

8

TOUR THE GALAXY

*T*he first stop on our galactic tour is the planet Veldin, a rocky desert world with few bodies of water. It's the place our hero, Ratchet, calls home. Life is simple on Veldin, but it isn't very exciting. That all changes for Ratchet when a curious little robot crash-lands near his home, warning of an impending attack on the Galactic Rangers.

KYZIL PLATEAU

The Kyzil Plateau region is one of the major population centers on Veldin. Natural wildlife includes Horny Toads and Skreeducks, both of which are known to attack if provoked. Thankfully, they can easily be scared away with a quick whack of an OmniWrench. Ratchet knows every inch of this area like the back of his hand, and he loves to go joyriding on its vast open plains.

GRIM'S WORKSHOP

Grim's Workshop on the Kyzil Plateau is where most residents come for spaceship repairs. This has been Ratchet's home ever since he was left on its doorstep as a baby. His room is high up in the rafters, which he reaches using his swingshot.

*T*he planet Quartu is the home of Chairman Drek and the Blarg. Quartu's environment has been ruined by massive amounts of pollution generated from the many factories created by Drek Industries. In fact, Quartu is the number one emitter of poisonous gases in its solar system.

Skorg City is perpetually shrouded in darkness, thanks to the massive plumes of smoke emitted from its many factories. It is the headquarters of Drek Industries, the place where Chairman Drek plots all of his evil schemes.

WARBOT FACTORY

The warbot factory on Skorg City builds, not surprisingly, warbots. It was designed and created by Dr. Nefarious for Chairman Drek to build a robot army capable of destroying the Galactic Rangers. It's also the birthplace of pint-sized hero Clank, who was created during a freak electrical storm that temporarily shorted out the factory's computer and changed the robot's programming.

8

TOUR THE GALAXY

Shortly after departing from Veldin to warn the Galactic Rangers of Drek's impending attack, Ratchet and Clank crash-land on the planet Novalis. Full of lush greenery and beautiful waterways, Novalis is home to millions of peaceful inhabitants.

NOVALIS IS HOME TO 7,257 DIFFERENT TYPES OF INSECTS.

NOVALIS VALLEY

Ratchet and Clank set down for repairs in Novalis Valley, but find Drek's forces have followed them and are attacking the nearby town. Battling through waves of warbots and Blarg, the duo finds the town's mayor locked inside his own ship! Our heroes free the mayor, who informs them that his nephew, hoverboard champion Skidd McMarx, is in trouble on the planet Aridia.

WATERWORKS

Novalis has one of the most complex sewer networks in the galaxy. Ratchet and Clank make their way through these Waterworks to find The Plumber, the only person on Novalis with the skill to repair their spaceship.

8

TOUR THE GALAXY

Aridia is a world filled with dangerous beauty, where twinkling purple skies hang over a landscape of bubbling mud and schools of vicious sandsharks. Ratchet and Clank take a detour to Aridia after learning that Skidd McMarx, one of Ratchet's heroes, is in some serious trouble.

SANDSHARK VALLEY

Ratchet and Clank find Skidd surrounded by sandsharks in the appropriately named Sandshark Valley. Sandsharks are nasty little creatures that like to bury themselves up to the fin in sand as they "swim" around in the loose earth and pop up to feed on unsuspecting prey. Luckily, Ratchet is able to save Skidd by bashing all of the sandsharks with his OmniWrench. As a way of saying thanks, Skidd gives Ratchet his personal hoverboard!

SKIDD'S STORE

As it turns out, Skidd McMarx was visiting Aridia to check on the construction of his new sporting goods store/extreme sports arena. Ratchet and Clank head inside to clear the place of sandsharks—only to discover that parts of the building are totally flooded. Good thing somebody left a Hyrdodisplacer nearby, allowing Ratchet and Clank to drain the water and finish their job.

8

TOUR THE GALAXY

Kerwan is the hub for all major activity in the universe and the home of the legendary Galactic Rangers. You can find life forms from all over the galaxy on this planet, all of them trying to live in peace and earn a living. Ratchet and Clank arrive too late to warn the Galactic Rangers of Drek's warbot attack, but they're just in time to save the day!

ALEERO CITY

Aleero City is the bustling capital of Kerwan, full of high-speed hovercars and bright neon advertisements. Normally a peaceful, if not fast-paced, metropolis, life in Aleero City is quickly upended by the invasion of the Blarg. After dispatching the warbots using the Magnebooster built into their ship, Ratchet and Clank patrol the city to mop up the rest of Drek's forces.

GALACTIC RANGERS HQ

A shining beacon of justice, the Galactic Rangers Headquarters lies at the center of Aleero City. Here, Captain Qwark and the other Rangers keep an eye on events across the galaxy. It's also where all of their custom gadgets and weapons are built.

TOUR THE GALAXY

The far-off planet of Rilgar is famous for two things: its championship hoverboard course and thriving underground weapons market. With his newly acquired official Skidd McMarx hoverboard, Ratchet leaps at the opportunity to show his stuff in front of a crowd.

BLACKWATER CITY

The environment on Rilgar causes the water to appear black, hence the name "Blackwater City." Although Ratchet and Clank travel here to enter the city's hoverboard races, they discover that Drek's forces have already set up shop in the city streets.

After dispatching their foes, the duo meets a shady black market vendor who tells them about the RYNO: a weapon of mass destruction that can only be built if someone finds nine special Holocards hidden throughout the galaxy. As an incentive to track down the Holocards, the vendor gives Ratchet a Trespasser: a perfect device for breaking into computer-controlled locks.

HOVERBOARD COURSE

The Blackwater City hoverboard course, designed by the legendary hoverboard champion RJ Dixion, is full of tight turns and wicked jumps. Ratchet skillfully dodges his opponents, leaps through shortcuts, and performs some wicked stunts to claim first place. His reward: more bolts than you can shake a Lombax tail at!

NEBULA G34 »

After leaving Rilgar, Ratchet and Clank head to Nebula G34, where rumor has it the Blarg are working on some sort of secret weapon. They arrive to discover a massive space station and a Blarg warship hidden among the asteroids and cosmic dust of the nebula.

BLARG TACTICAL STATION

Once inside the station, Ratchet and Clank immediately begin to search for the secret Blarg weapon. Clank explores the exterior of the station on his own, discovering a Gadgebot upgrade chip that allows him to control any Gadgebot he finds. Breaking into the nearby Blarg Warship, Clank picks up a pair of Magneboots for Ratchet and returns to the station.

Reunited, the duo begins traversing deeper into the facility, using the Trespasser to hack through the station's security systems. The Blarg scramble to stop our heroes, but are no match for Ratchet's superior gun skills. Ratchet and Clank soon discover the secret Blarg weapon: the Predator Rocket Launcher! However, escaping wouldn't prove as simple as breaking in.

BLARGIAN SNAGGLEBEAST

During their escape, Ratchet and Clank enter a huge, lava-filled chamber, where they face the Blarg's other secret weapon: the Blargian Snagglebeast. This massive creature has been outfitted with a control device that allows the Blarg to command it from their control booth. The Blargian Snagglebeast has razor-sharp teeth and can shoot fireballs from its hands!

TOUR THE GALAXY

Gaspar is the hottest and steamiest planet in the galaxy, thanks to the massive fields of lava that cover its surface. As unlivable as that sounds, it didn't stop Dr. Nefarious from building a secret facility on the few areas of stable ground on the planet. Ratchet and Clank arrive to find the area full of well-armed Blarg, but what are a few bad guys and a deadly floor of lava to two of the greatest heroes in the galaxy?

LAVA FIELDS

The ground on Gaspar is literally lava, meaning Ratchet and Clank have to carefully watch their step while exploring the Blarg facilities. The pair discovers that this area also serves a Blarg depot, where much of their latest weapons and equipment are constructed and distributed to Blarg forces across the galaxy.

It turns out not all of the Blarg are bad. Ratchet and Clank find a Blarg "scientist" on the outskirts of the facility. He agrees to give Ratchet and Clank a jet pack upgrade if they can help him collect Telepathopus brains for his "studies" into telepathy.

THE TELEPATHOPUS

The Telepathopus is a massive creature built mostly of brain tissue. It can levitate using only its mind and attacks potential enemies with several tentacles that hang from its body. The biggest Telepathopuses are found in the outskirts of the lava fields.

A Telepathopus starts life as a brain inside a gelatinous egg, which Ratchet can quickly break open using his OmniWrench. Collecting their brains is super gross, but Ratchet and Clank find it's well worth it to fly around with that sweet, sweet jet pack.

TOUR THE GALAXY

8

Pokitaru is a gorgeous planet comprised of thousands of tropical islands. Creatures from all over the galaxy come here to rest, relax, and take a break from work. The biggest slacker on the island is Felton Razz, Grim's brother, who came to Pokitaru for a fishing trip ten years ago and never left!

Ratchet and Clank arrive on Pokitaru to find the Blarg commanding huge Hydroharvesters, trying to suck up all the clean water on the planet. The Hydroharvesters are built from materials that make them invincible against the rockets equipped on Ratchet's ship.

Luckily, Big Al happens to be on the planet for a comic book convention. He is able to use his super smarts to upgrade Ratchet's ship with Tesla Blast Rockets that easily take down the Blarg Hydroharvesters.

JOWAI RESORT

The Jowai Resort is one of the premier vacation spots on Pokitaru. Surrounded by picturesque islands, visitors at the Jowai Resort can enjoy swimming in its pristine waters or just hang out in the Tiki juice bar with a cold beverage.

8

B atalia is an icy planet in the Solana star system where the Starwatch Defense Cannon, one of the galaxy's greatest defense systems, is located. Shortly after leaving Gaspar, Ratchet and Clank receive a distress call from the Galactic Rangers: Batalia is under attack from the Blarg!

FORT KRONTOS

Fort Krontos was built to house and defend the Starwatch Defense Cannon. Its huge walls and batteries of laser cannons were meant to fight off any force that attempted to get inside. The Blarg prove to be very resourceful, however, and shoot huge holes in its defenses. They would have succeeded in stealing the cannon had Ratchet and Clank not arrived on the scene.

STARWATCH DEFENSE CANNON

The Starwatch Defense Cannon is thought to be the most powerful ion blaster in the universe. Its gigantic cannon can take down massive warships in a single shot! After fighting off the Blarg's ground forces, Ratchet and Clank get a chance to test-drive this puppy, taking out several Blarg capital ships and putting a huge dent in Drek's army.

TOUR THE GALAXY

Kalebo III is most famous for being the home of Gadgetron, makers of fine weaponry and useful gadgets. Of course, Chairman Drek wants all of their technology for himself and sends his goons to take over Gadgetron Headquarters. Ratchet and Clank have to fight off waves of Blarg snipers and Warbots before the area is secure, earning them the gratitude of Gadgetron CEO Wendell Lumos.

GADGETRON HQ

The Gadgetron Headquarters takes up a huge chunk of real estate on Kalebo III. In their many research facilities, the eggheads at Gadgetron create and test all sorts of strange devices. Ratchet finds the Map-o-Matic upgrade while exploring Gadgetron, and he uses it to uncover all of the hidden Golden Bolts and raritanium on the planets he's previously visited.

Gadgetron even has its own hoverboard course and sponsors a tournament at its headquarters. Although far tougher to navigate than the course in Blackwater City, Ratchet uses his superb hoverboard skills to smoke the competition. As a reward, Wendell Lumos gives Ratchet the experimental Hologuise, which Ratchet can use to sneak about the Deplanetizer and, hopefully, destroy it from the inside.

THE DEPLANETIZER ≫

Tho Deplanetizer is a space station with the biggest, meanest, nastiest weapon the galaxy has ever seen. Its massive laser cannon can destroy entire planets faster than you can say "ham sandwich." It is the key component to Chairman Drek's master plan: rather than cleaning up the pollution on his own planet, Drek uses the Deplanetizer to blow up better and cleaner planets and takes the best pieces to assemble an entirely new world called "New Quartu."

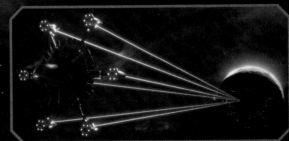

Dr. Nefarious, a mad scientist with a sinister plan of his own, built this massive planet-shattering facility. While pretending to work for Chairman Drek, Nefarious takes over the Deplanetizer and focuses its beam on a nearby star. If allowed to fire, the Deplanetizer would cause the star to become a supernova and destroy all life in the solar system!

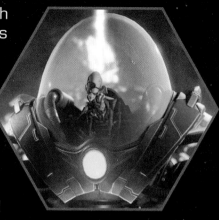

Against all odds, Ratchet and Clank sneak onboard the Deplanetizer by using the Hologuise to pose as the traitorous Captain Qwark. They make their way to the core of the facility and damage the Deplanetizer's stabilizer systems, forcing it to miss the sun entirely.

Dr. Nefarious, now furious, tries to get revenge on Ratchet and Clank by fighting them inside a massive mechanical suit! Our heroes use every tool at their disposal to take down Dr. Nefarious, escaping just moments before the Deplanetizer crashes onto New Quartu. The galaxy was once again at peace, and the rest, as they say, is history.

SECTION 9
LEARN THE LANGUAGE
OF THE UNIVERSE

As you've read through this book, you might have noticed some words written in an alien language. Normally it would take a team of scientists years of research to decipher the meaning behind these strange symbols, but all you need is this book!

The tables below show you how the symbols of the alien language line up with the English alphabet. This book has several pages with hidden messages written with these symbols. Grab a pencil and a piece of scrap paper, and see if you can decode them all!

Note: Exclamation marks (!), question marks (?), apostrophes ('), and quotation marks (") are the same as our language.

Names

ᒥᐱᒣᑕᕼᐱᒣ
= RATCHET

ᑕᒪᐱᕼᔦ
= CLANK

ᑕᐱᒣᒪᐱᐱᕼ ᔦᕼᐱᒣᕼᔦ
= CAPTAIN QWARK

ᔦᒣ· ᕼᐱᔦᐱᒣᐱᔦᕼᒣᕼ
= DR. NEFARIOUS

Places

ᔦᐱᒪᔦᐱᕼ
= VELDIN

ᕼᔦᔦᐱᒪ ᒪᒪᕼᒣᐱᒣᕼ
= KYZIL PLATEAU

ᒪᒪᐱᐱᕼᔦ ᕼᒣᒣᔦ
= ALEERO CITY

ᔦᕼᐱᒣᒣᕼ
= QUARTU

ᒥᐱᒣᑕᕼᐱᒣ ᐱᕼᔦ ᑕᒪᐱᕼᔦ ᒣᕼᐱᔦᕼ
ᒣᒪᕼ ᐱᕼᒣ ᑕᒪᐱᒣᒥᐱᕼᒣ! ᒣᐱᒣᑕᕼᒣ ᒪᒣᕼ
ᕼᒣᐱᒣᔦᕼᕼᒣ ᒣᕼᒣᒣ ᒥᒣᒣᕼ!

LETTERS AND NUMBERS

ᗡ.	A	ⴽ	N	⅂	1
ⴺ	B	ᗺ	O	ⴺ	2
�	C	ⵕ.	P	ⴺ	3
ⴺ	D	ⵒ	Q	ⵗ	4
ⵦ	E	ⴽ	R	ⵦ	5
ⵦ	F	ᗷ	S	ⵦ	6
ⵦ	G	ⵕ.	T	ⵕ	7
ᗷ	H	ⵕⵕ	U	ᗺ	8
ⵦ	I	ⵗ	V	ⵗ	9
ⵕ	J	ⵦ	W	ⵕ	0
ⵦ	K	ⵦⵦ	X	'	.
ⵕ	L	ᗷ	Y	'	,
ⴽ	M	ⵦⵦ	Z		

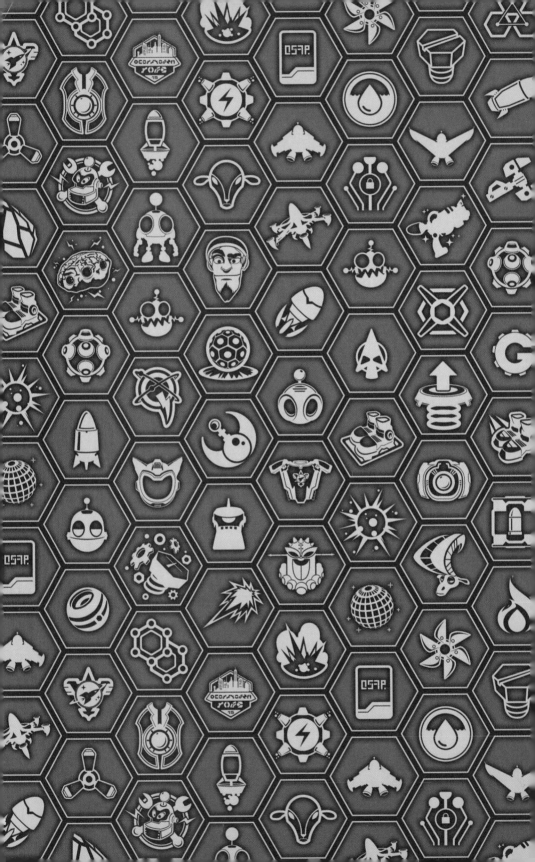